Judith Rossell

INSPECTOR STILTON
& the missing jewels

LITTLE HARE

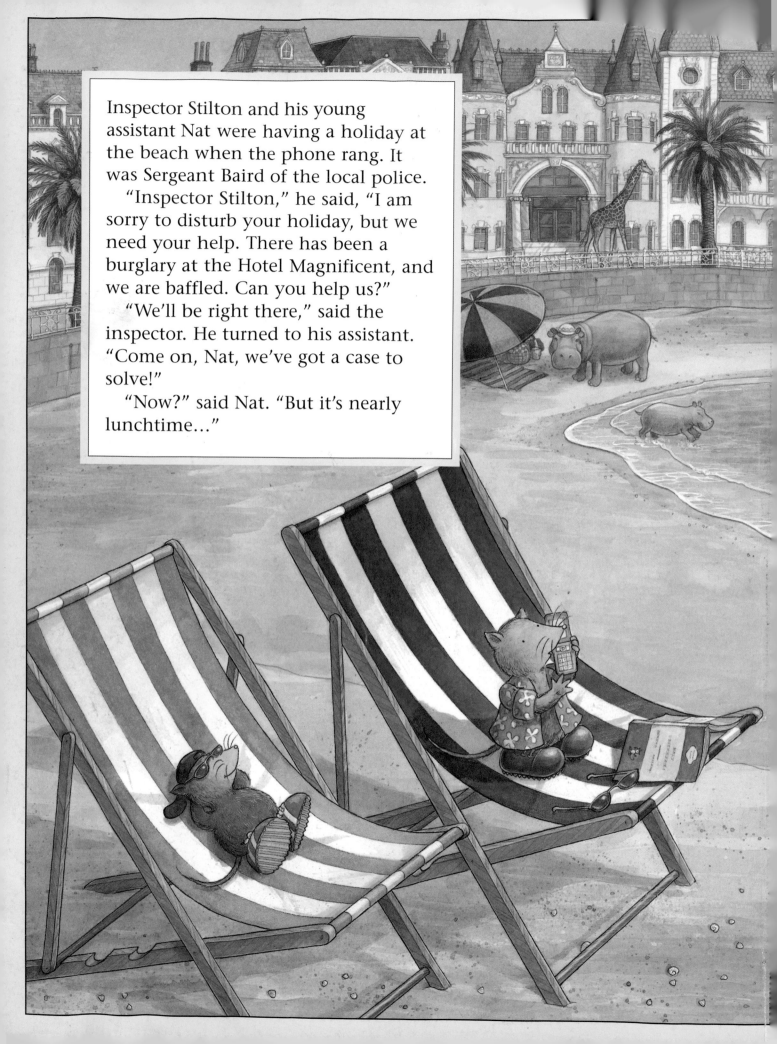

Inspector Stilton and his young assistant Nat were having a holiday at the beach when the phone rang. It was Sergeant Baird of the local police.

"Inspector Stilton," he said, "I am sorry to disturb your holiday, but we need your help. There has been a burglary at the Hotel Magnificent, and we are baffled. Can you help us?"

"We'll be right there," said the inspector. He turned to his assistant. "Come on, Nat, we've got a case to solve!"

"Now?" said Nat. "But it's nearly lunchtime…"

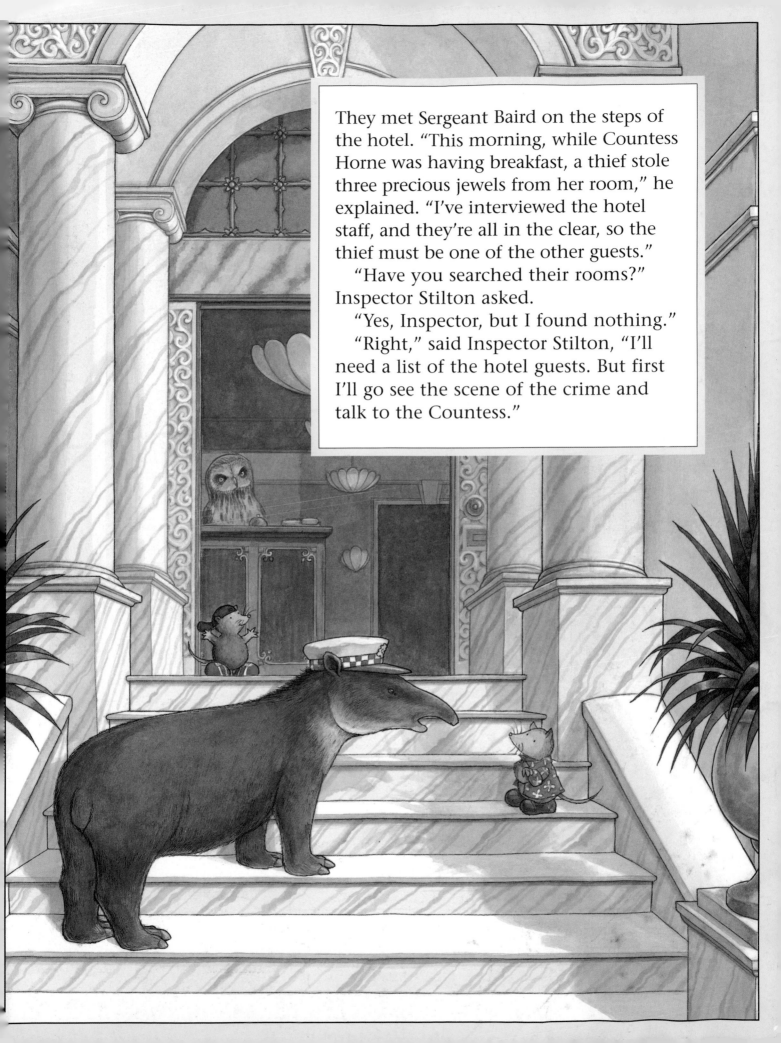

They met Sergeant Baird on the steps of the hotel. "This morning, while Countess Horne was having breakfast, a thief stole three precious jewels from her room," he explained. "I've interviewed the hotel staff, and they're all in the clear, so the thief must be one of the other guests."

"Have you searched their rooms?" Inspector Stilton asked.

"Yes, Inspector, but I found nothing."

"Right," said Inspector Stilton, "I'll need a list of the hotel guests. But first I'll go see the scene of the crime and talk to the Countess."

Room 1, Countess Horne

"Oh, Inspector!" cried Countess Horne. "My beautiful jewels were intact before breakfast, but look—while I was out three precious stones have been prised from this necklace and stolen. Please find them!"

Inspector Stilton gave a polite bow. "I'm afraid the three jewels could be hidden anywhere; we must keep our eyes open. Luckily, there is something in this room that shows me exactly what they look like."

"Let's start looking straight after lunch," suggested Nat. "Did you notice the ten strawberries in here?"

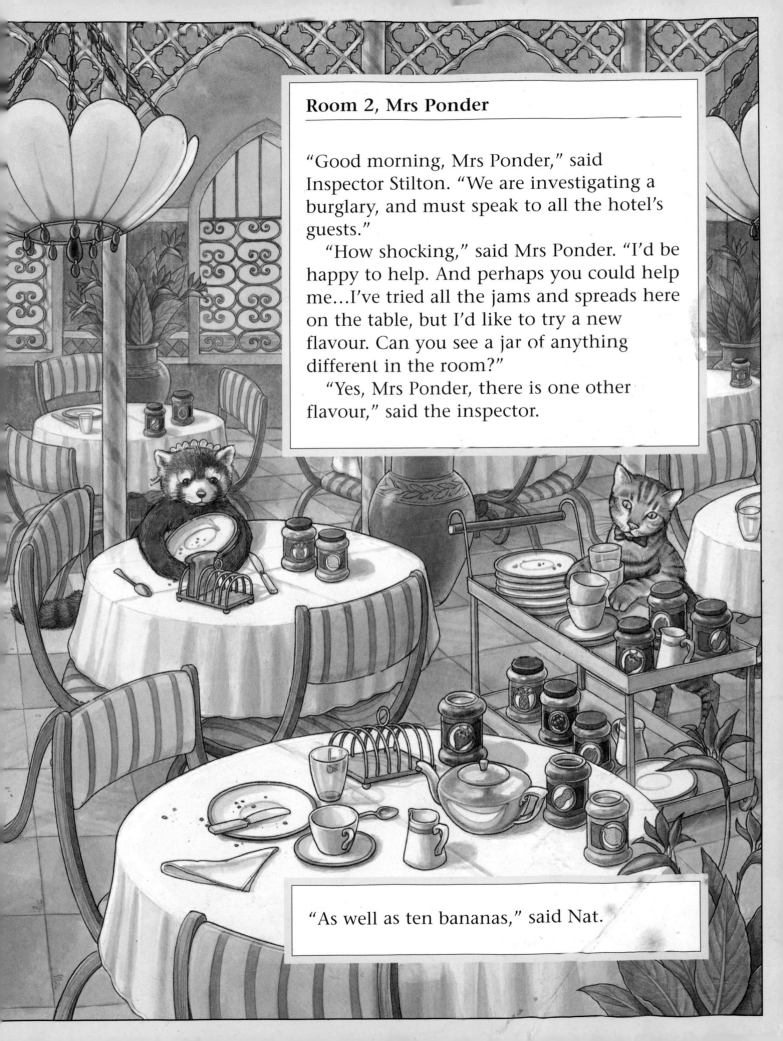

Room 2, Mrs Ponder

"Good morning, Mrs Ponder," said Inspector Stilton. "We are investigating a burglary, and must speak to all the hotel's guests."

"How shocking," said Mrs Ponder. "I'd be happy to help. And perhaps you could help me…I've tried all the jams and spreads here on the table, but I'd like to try a new flavour. Can you see a jar of anything different in the room?"

"Yes, Mrs Ponder, there is one other flavour," said the inspector.

"As well as ten bananas," said Nat.

Room 3, Colonel Carp

"Fifty laps, every morning," said Colonel Carp. "You should swim, Inspector. Build up your muscles. But Mr Tiler has a problem that needs brains, not muscles. He has to fix this broken mosaic—and we can't work out which three pieces he should use."

"That's just the kind of puzzle I'm good at," said Inspector Stilton.

"And I can't work out why there are ten ice-cream cones in here," said Nat.

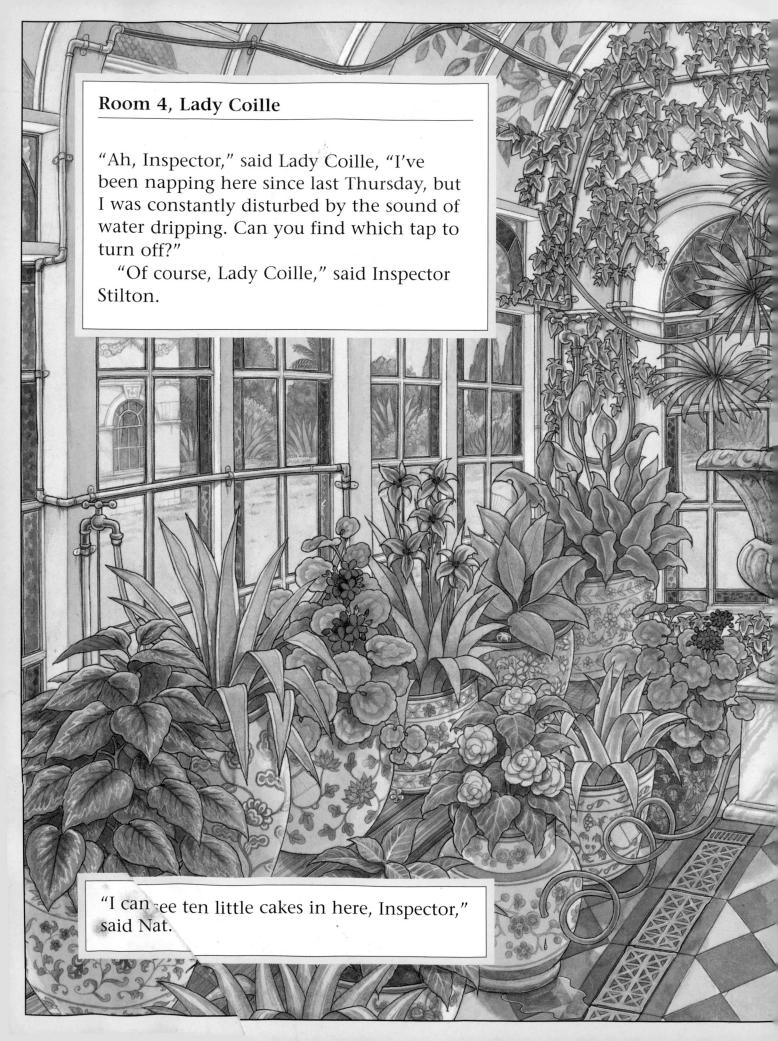

Room 4, Lady Coille

"Ah, Inspector," said Lady Coille, "I've been napping here since last Thursday, but I was constantly disturbed by the sound of water dripping. Can you find which tap to turn off?"

"Of course, Lady Coille," said Inspector Stilton.

"I can see ten little cakes in here, Inspector," said Nat.

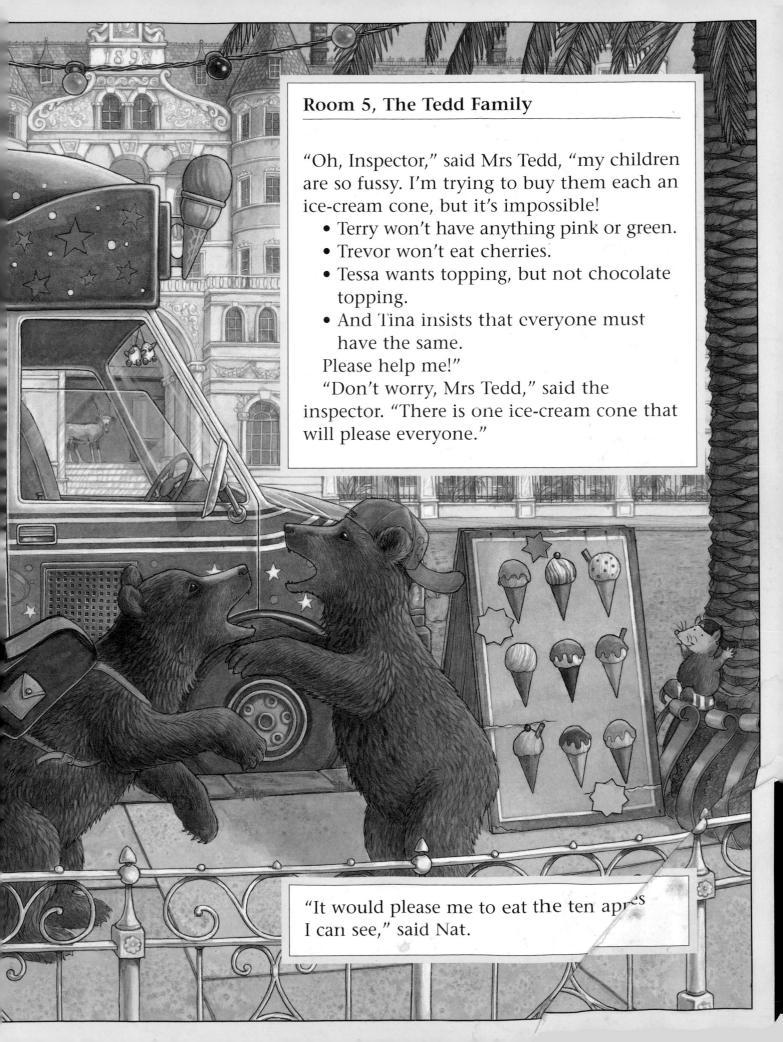

Room 5, The Tedd Family

"Oh, Inspector," said Mrs Tedd, "my children are so fussy. I'm trying to buy them each an ice-cream cone, but it's impossible!
- Terry won't have anything pink or green.
- Trevor won't eat cherries.
- Tessa wants topping, but not chocolate topping.
- And Tina insists that everyone must have the same.

Please help me!"

"Don't worry, Mrs Tedd," said the inspector. "There is one ice-cream cone that will please everyone."

"It would please me to eat the ten ap̄rḛs I can see," said Nat.

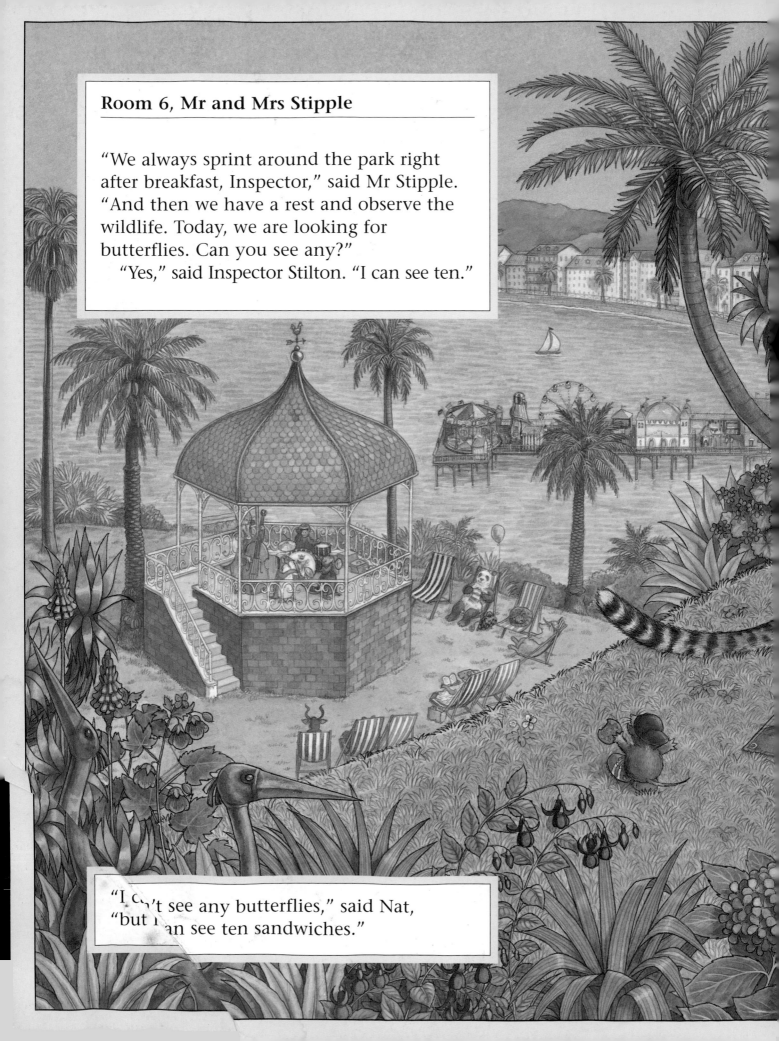

Room 6, Mr and Mrs Stipple

"We always sprint around the park right after breakfast, Inspector," said Mr Stipple. "And then we have a rest and observe the wildlife. Today, we are looking for butterflies. Can you see any?"

"Yes," said Inspector Stilton. "I can see ten."

"I can't see any butterflies," said Nat, "but I can see ten sandwiches."

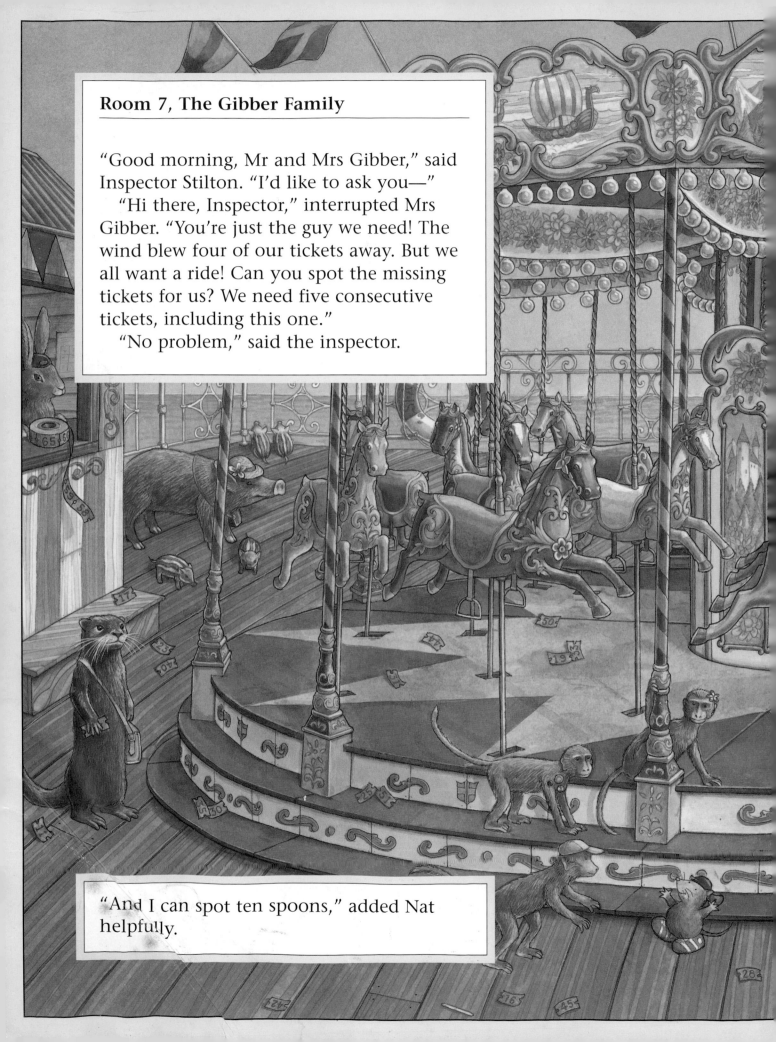

Room 7, The Gibber Family

"Good morning, Mr and Mrs Gibber," said Inspector Stilton. "I'd like to ask you—"

"Hi there, Inspector," interrupted Mrs Gibber. "You're just the guy we need! The wind blew four of our tickets away. But we all want a ride! Can you spot the missing tickets for us? We need five consecutive tickets, including this one."

"No problem," said the inspector.

"And I can spot ten spoons," added Nat helpfully.

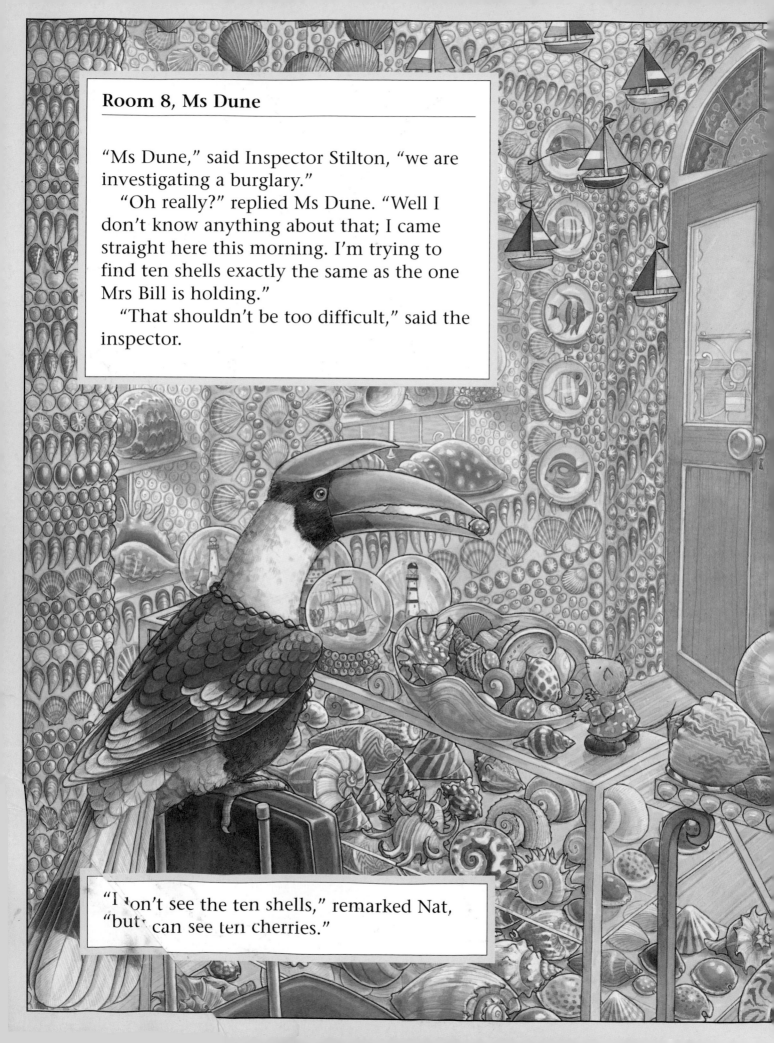

Room 8, Ms Dune

"Ms Dune," said Inspector Stilton, "we are investigating a burglary."

"Oh really?" replied Ms Dune. "Well I don't know anything about that; I came straight here this morning. I'm trying to find ten shells exactly the same as the one Mrs Bill is holding."

"That shouldn't be too difficult," said the inspector.

"I don't see the ten shells," remarked Nat, "but I can see ten cherries."

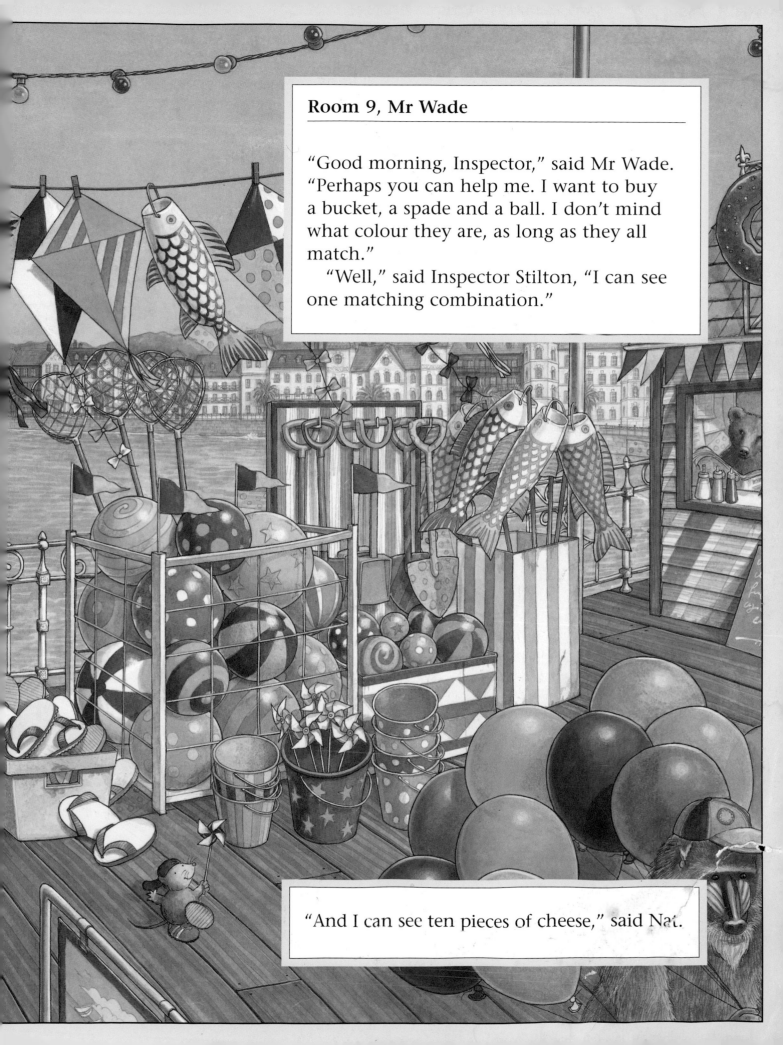

Room 9, Mr Wade

"Good morning, Inspector," said Mr Wade. "Perhaps you can help me. I want to buy a bucket, a spade and a ball. I don't mind what colour they are, as long as they all match."

"Well," said Inspector Stilton, "I can see one matching combination."

"And I can see ten pieces of cheese," said Nat.

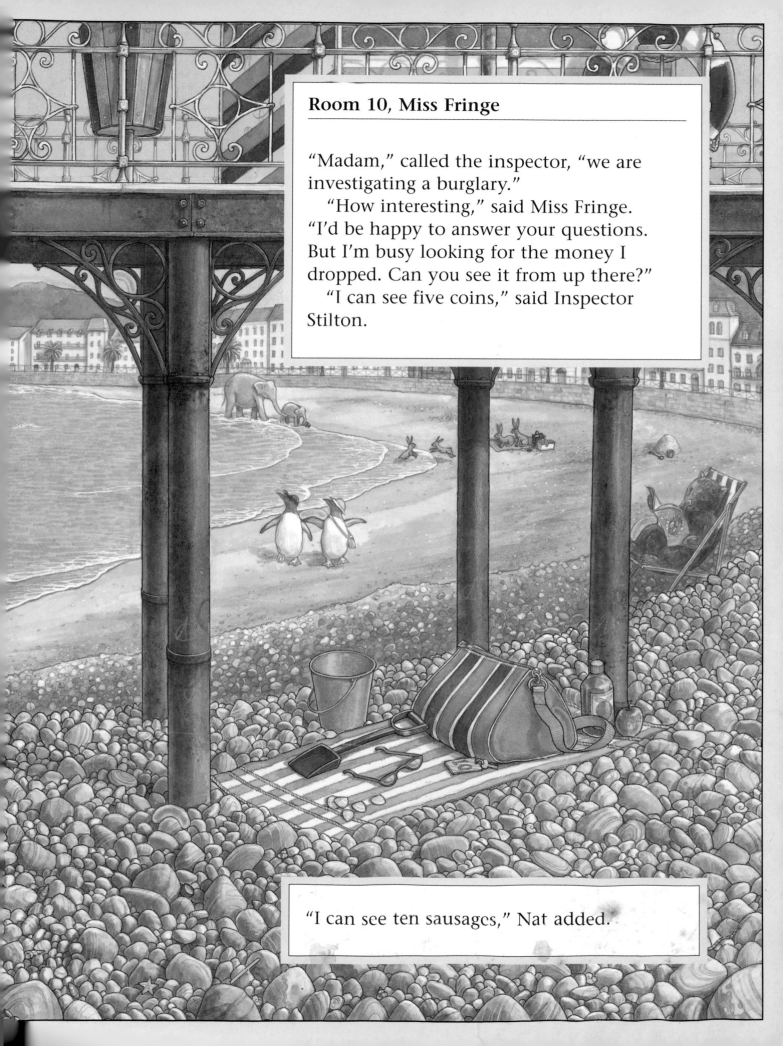

Room 10, Miss Fringe

"Madam," called the inspector, "we are investigating a burglary."

"How interesting," said Miss Fringe. "I'd be happy to answer your questions. But I'm busy looking for the money I dropped. Can you see it from up there?"

"I can see five coins," said Inspector Stilton.

"I can see ten sausages," Nat added.

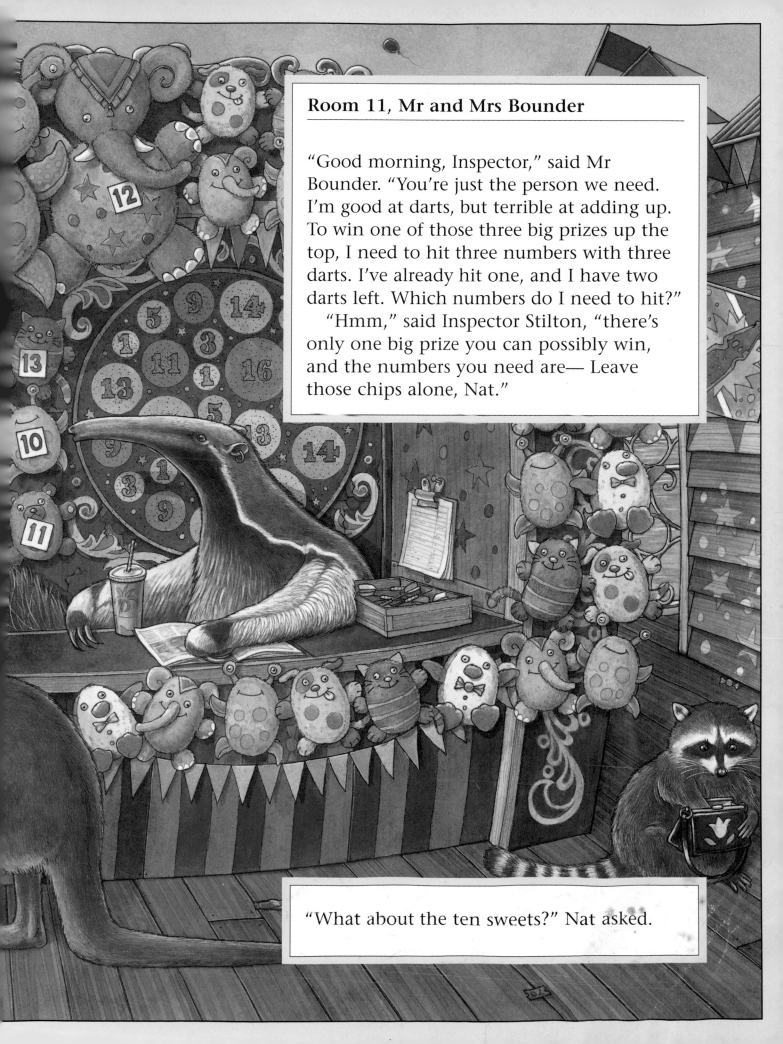

Room 11, Mr and Mrs Bounder

"Good morning, Inspector," said Mr Bounder. "You're just the person we need. I'm good at darts, but terrible at adding up. To win one of those three big prizes up the top, I need to hit three numbers with three darts. I've already hit one, and I have two darts left. Which numbers do I need to hit?"

"Hmm," said Inspector Stilton, "there's only one big prize you can possibly win, and the numbers you need are— Leave those chips alone, Nat."

"What about the ten sweets?" Nat asked.

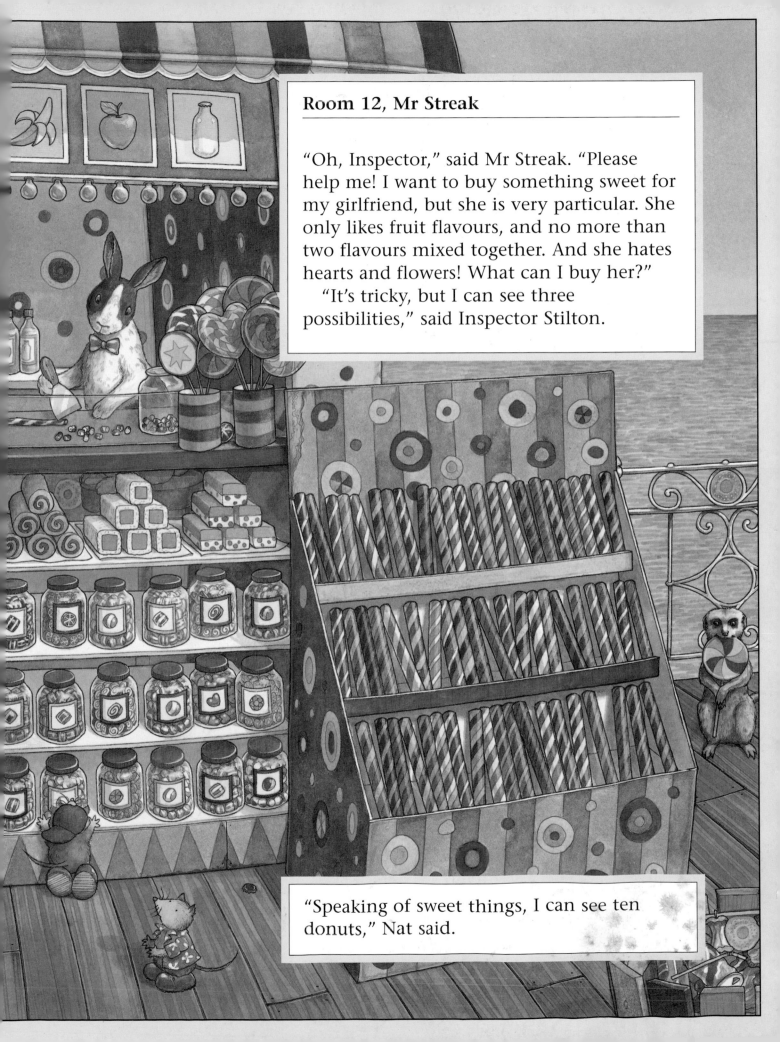

Room 12, Mr Streak

"Oh, Inspector," said Mr Streak. "Please help me! I want to buy something sweet for my girlfriend, but she is very particular. She only likes fruit flavours, and no more than two flavours mixed together. And she hates hearts and flowers! What can I buy her?"

"It's tricky, but I can see three possibilities," said Inspector Stilton.

"Speaking of sweet things, I can see ten donuts," Nat said.

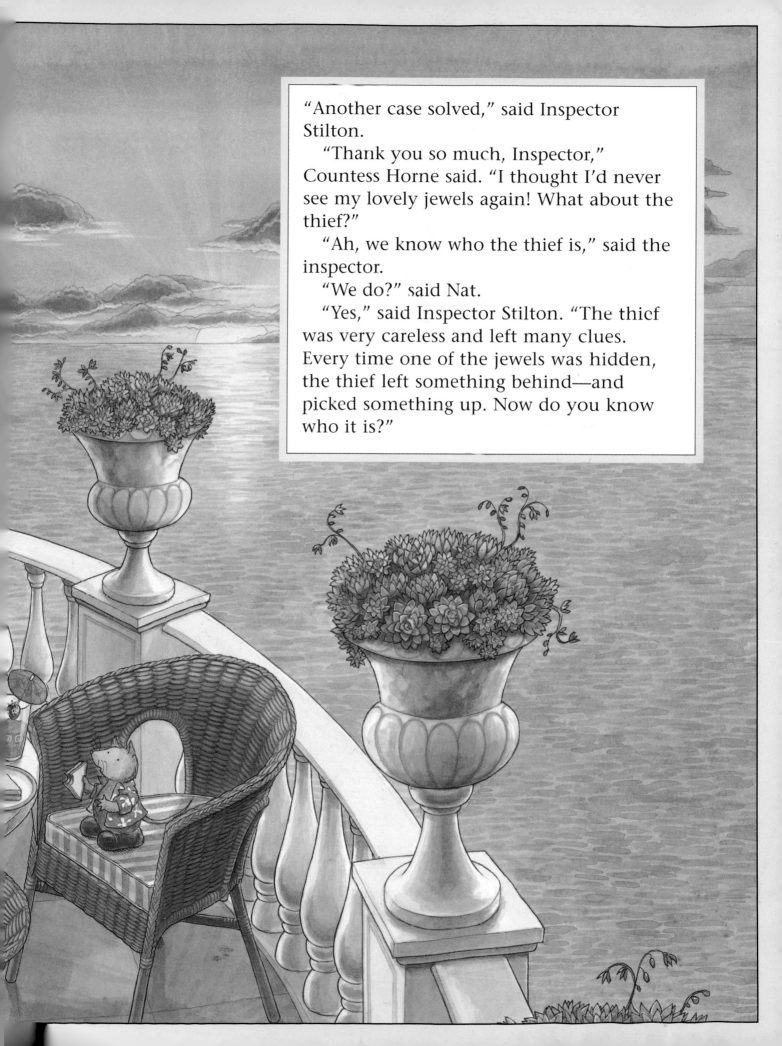

"Another case solved," said Inspector Stilton.

"Thank you so much, Inspector," Countess Horne said. "I thought I'd never see my lovely jewels again! What about the thief?"

"Ah, we know who the thief is," said the inspector.

"We do?" said Nat.

"Yes," said Inspector Stilton. "The thief was very careless and left many clues. Every time one of the jewels was hidden, the thief left something behind—and picked something up. Now do you know who it is?"

SEARCH • SEEK • SOLVE • SOLUTIONS

● The puzzle solved by Inspector Stilton
○ The hidden shapes spotted by Nat (there are actually 11, not 10!)

Room 1, Countess Horne

Room 2, Mrs Ponder

Room 3, Colonel Carp

Room 4, Lady Coille

Room 5, The Tedd Family

Room 6, Mr and Mrs Stipple

- The three missing jewels
- Evidence left or collected by the thief in each scene she visited

Room 7, The Gibber Family

Room 8, Ms Dune

Room 9, Mr Wade

Room 10, Miss Fringe

Room 11, Mr and Mrs Bounder

Room 12, Mr Streak

For Ruth—JR

Acknowledgments
A big thank you to Christopher and Annie,
Stephen, Hazel, and Sally-Ann and Lily

Little Hare Books
4/21 Mary Street, Surry Hills
NSW 2010 AUSTRALIA

www.littleharebooks.com

First published in 2005
Reprinted in 2006

National Library of Australia
Cataloguing-in-Publication entry

Rossell, Judith.
Inspector Stilton and the missing jewels.

For children.
ISBN 1 921049 09 X.

1. Puzzles - Juvenile literature. I. Title.
793.73

Designed by WideOpen.net.au
Produced by Phoenix Offset, Hong Kong
Printed in China

5 4 3 2